POCAHONTAS

FACILITATING EXCHANGE BETWEEN THE POWHATAN AND THE JAMESTOWN SETTLERS

WOMEN WHO CHANGED HISTORY

POCAHONTAS

FACILITATING EXCHANGE BETWEEN THE POWHATAN AND THE JAMESTOWN SETTLERS

JEANNE NAGLE

Britannica Educational Publishing

IN ASSOCIATION WITH

ROSEN EDUCATIONAL SERVICES

Published in 2018 by Britannica Educational Publishing (a trademark of Encyclopædia Britannica, Inc.) in association with The Rosen Publishing Group, Inc.
29 East 21st Street, New York, NY 10010

Distributed exclusively by Rosen Publishing.
To see additional Britannica Educational Publishing titles, go to rosenpublishing.com.

First Edition

Britannica Educational Publishing
J.E. Luebering: Executive Director, Core Editorial
Andrea R. Field: Managing Editor, Compton's by Britannica

Rosen Publishing
Heather Moore Niver: Editor
Nelson Sá: Art Director
Michael Moy: Designer
Cindy Reiman: Photography Manager
Heather Moore Niver: Photo Researcher

Library of Congress Cataloging-in-Publication Data

Names: Nagle, Jeanne, author.
Title: Pocahontas : facilitating exchange between the Powhatan and the Jamestown settlers / Jeanne Nagle.
Description: New York, NY : Britannica Educational Publishing, 2018. | Series: Women who changed history | Audience: Grades 5-8. | Includes bibliographical references and index.
Identifiers: LCCN 2017001517 | ISBN 9781680486551 (library bound book : alk. paper) | ISBN 9781680486537 (pbk. book : alk. paper) | ISBN 9781680486544 (6 pack : alk. paper)
Subjects: LCSH: Pocahontas, -1617—Juvenile literature. | Powhatan women—Biography—Juvenile literature. | Powhatan Indians—History—Juvenile literature. | Smith, John, 1580-1631—Juvenile literature. | Jamestown (Va.)—History—Juvenile literature. | Jamestown (Va.)—Biography—Juvenile literature. | Virginia—History—Colonial period, ca. 1600-1775—Juvenile literature.
Classification: LCC E99.P85 N34 2018 | DDC 975.501092 [B] —dc23
LC record available at https://lccn.loc.gov/2017001517

Manufactured in the United States of America

Photo credits: Cover Print Collector/Hulton Archive/Getty Images; p. 7 MPI/Archive Photos /Getty Images; p. 9 Lives of Famous Indian Chiefs by Norman B. Wood., 1906; p. 11 Library of Congress Prints and Photograph Division; pp. 12–13 SuperStock; p. 14 Stephen Saks Photography/Alamy Stock Photo; p. 17 alekseykh/iStock/Thinkstock; p. 19 JPTenor/Alamy Stock Photo; pp. 21, 29 Virginia Historical Society, Richmond, Virginia, USA/Bridgeman Images; p. 23 SuperStock/Getty Images; pp. 24–25 MixPix/Alamy Stock Photo; p. 26 Library of Congress, Washington, D.C. (Digital File Number: LC-DIG-pga-03343); p. 30 Hulton Archive/Hulton Royals Collection/Getty Images; p. 31 Universal History Archive/Universal Images Group/Getty Images; p. 33 Kean Collection/Archive Photos/Getty Images; pp. 34–35 Peter Cripps/Alamy Stock Photo; p. 37 Three Lions/Hulton Royals Collection/Getty Images; p. 39 Universal Images Group/Getty Images; p. 40 Everett Collection, Inc./Alamy Stock Photo; pp. 42–43 Historic Map Works LLC/Getty Images.

CONTENTS

INTRODUCTION

In the spring of 1606, King James I of England granted a charter to the Virginia Company of London. The charter granted to the company the rights to settle, explore, and govern limited parts of the New World. On December 20 of that year, an expedition of about one hundred men sailed from London. Five months later, they anchored their three small ships—the *Godspeed*, the *Discovery*, and the *Susan Constant*—off the coast of a marshy peninsula 30 miles (48 kilometers) up the James River, in what is now the state of Virginia.

There they established the first permanent English settlement in America, Jamestown, named after King James. The location they had chosen appeared to have many advantages. For instance, their ships could pull up close to it in deep water, for easy loading and unloading. Also, it was easy to defend. Unfortunately, the site was low, damp, swampy, and unhealthful. A combination of bad water from the river and disease-bearing mosquitoes sickened the settlers, and many soon died. Famine, caused by limited food supplies, added to the settlers' difficulties in the early months of Jamestown's founding.

At the same time, in the same general area, a young Native American princess named Matoaka was learning how to be a young woman of her tribe. Nicknamed Pocahontas, which means "playful one" in her native language, she was a younger daughter of Powhatan, chief of a federation of Algonquian Indian tribes. As a young girl of ten or eleven, Pocahontas would have been taught how to grow

After issues of distrust were calmed, the Jamestown settlers often traded with the Powhatan, a nearby Native American tribe. One of the regulars during these meetings was a young Pocahontas.

and collect food, which, in addition to whatever game the men hunted, kept the tribe fed.

Before long, the two groups would be forced to cross paths. Pocahontas first became acquainted with the colonists who settled in the Chesapeake Bay area in 1607. A familiar story tells how she saved the life of Jamestown settler Captain John Smith. Many historians doubt that the incident took place—at least not in the way Smith told the story. Regardless, many other accounts by Smith and his fellow settlers make clear Pocahontas did have a relationship with the people of Jamestown. As a youngster she came along when members of her tribe went to the settlement to conduct trade. The Native Americans brought corn and other food to the hungry colonists, who gave them beads and other items in return. A bit later, she would lead such visits as a representative of her father.

Pocahontas's relationship with the Jamestown colonists was complicated. There were times when her attempts to help the English put her in conflict with her own tribe, particularly her father. Usually the colonists were grateful. But sometimes they took advantage of her kindness. One Englishman kidnapped Pocahontas and kept her until her father gave the settlers what they wanted.

The world will probably never know why Pocahontas felt the need to help the strangers who had invaded her homeland. But without her help and that of her tribe, Jamestown may have vanished and the settlers returned to England. An important piece of American history could have been lost forever were it not for Pocahontas.

CHAPTER ONE

A YOUNG PRINCESS LEADS THE WAY

Historians do not know what day Pocahontas was born, and they are not even sure of the exact year. Most guesses put her birthday in or around 1596. She was the daughter of a powerful Native American chief named Powhatan. At the peak of his power, Powhatan is estimated to have ruled between thirteen thousand and thirty-four thousand people. He presided over an empire named for him at the time the English established the Jamestown Colony.

Sketch depicting Powhatan, chief of a Native American confederacy that bore his name. Pocahontas was rumored to be his favorite daughter.

Little is known about her mother, who was one of Powhatan's numerous wives.

The chief was the father to many children, but some people believe that Pocahontas was among his very favorites.

STRANGERS ON THE SHORE

The fact that her nickname could also be translated to "mischievous one" indicates that Pocahontas was a curious child who liked adventure. Naturally, then, she was terribly inquisitive when she discovered that men from another land had sailed into the bay and were setting up a village nearby.

Among those men was Captain John Smith, a member of the Virginia Company and one of the seven members of the Jamestown Colony's governing council. Shortly after arriving in what is now Virginia, Smith began a series of river voyages that later enabled him to draw a remarkably accurate map of the area. While exploring the Chickahominy River in December 1607, he and his party were attacked by members of the Powhatan empire. Smith was captured by Powhatan's younger brother, Opechancanough, and brought before the chief himself.

What happened next is a long-lasting legend that has been passed down for generations.

SAVING JOHN SMITH

According to the story, Powhatan's warriors were about to put Smith to death. Smith claims that Pocahontas, who

This full-color lithograph portrait is of Captain John Smith, the English settler who appears to have played a pivotal role in the story of the Indian princess Pocahontas.

Captain Smith may have misunderstood the intentions of the tribe when he was brought before Chief Powhatan. Then again, the entire incident may never have happened at all.

was about ten or eleven, placed herself between him and his executioners, then pleaded with her father to spare him. Apparently moved by his daughter's words and actions, Powhatan gave in, and Smith was allowed to go free.

Many historians doubt that the incident took place. Smith failed to include it in his first published account of Virginia, though he mentioned Pocahontas's visits to Jamestown. Only much later did he include the story in his *Generall Historie of Virginia* (1624). Some people think that Smith may have misunderstood Powhatan's intentions. What he believed to be an execution was perhaps instead a test of Smith's courage or an adoption ceremony welcoming him to the tribe. Others have said that he invented Pocahontas's rescue as an exciting story to tell about life in the New World.

A FINE REPRESENTATIVE

Even if Pocahontas did not save Smith's life in that instance, she did play a part in helping him and the other colonists survive. Soon after Smith was released by Powhatan and he had returned to Jamestown, a ship carrying food and supplies arrived. The residents of Jamestown were thrilled, because their stockpile had gotten dangerously low. Unfortunately, a fire swept through the colony on January 7, 1608, burning everything in its path—including most of the rations that had just come off the ship.

A view from inside the re-creation of James Fort, which protected the residents of Jamestown. The site is open to the public as a living history museum.

When Powhatan learned about the fire, he sent members of his tribe with gifts of deer meat, fish, and bread. One of those who brought the food was Pocahontas. This and subsequent visits to the colony were not just about being a representative of her father. The young princess's curiosity about the English and their way of life had not dimmed one bit. She enjoyed spending time speaking with Smith, who was learning her Algonquin language. Still a child, she also liked turning cartwheels and playing games with the boys of the settlement.

As she grew older, Pocahontas also would accompany members of the tribe who were sent by Powhatan for other reasons. In the spring of 1608, she arrived at the colony with one of her father's advisers to negotiate the release of captured warriors. Smith agreed to release the men into her care. If one believes the story of how Pocahontas saved him the year before, it is easy to think he gave her the prisoners as payback. He even gave her a personal gift, most likely a handful of beads.

The young princess also came to Jamestown to make trade deals with the colonists. The native chief would offer Smith a share of whatever his people had stored for their own use. In return, he often asked for guns or swords. Sometimes Powhatan could be talked into accepting copper cooking pots or beads that he pretended were rare and valuable. Yet Powhatan never forgot his desire for weapons. Smith's constant refusals created tension between the two trading partners.

PEACE THROUGH STRENGTH

In his dealings with Native Americans, Smith's approach differed from those of the Spanish conquistadores who had arrived in the Americas about a century before. "Conquistador" is the name given to any of the leaders in the Spanish conquest of Latin America, especially Mexico and Peru, in the sixteenth century. They sailed to the Americas with certain goals in mind: to conquer the native peoples, to spread Christianity, and to look for gold and other treasure.

In many cases the conquistadores had brutally suppressed or killed thousands of native peoples. Instead, Smith chose to keep the Powhatan confederacy at bay through diplomacy and intimidation—not massacre. He believed the English could avoid bloodshed by projecting an image of strength.

A TIMELY WARNING

With more English citizens being transported to the Americas, the need for food within the colony continued to grow. By December of 1608, food rations in Jamestown were once again dangerously low. Trading with the Indians had come to a standstill over Smith's refusal to give them weapons. Yet the need for food was great, so Smith boarded a barge and took a party to Powhatan's village.

A bronze statue commemorating Pocahontas stands near a gate and greets visitors to the site of the original Jamestown settlement.

Earlier the chief had sent a message that, in exchange for building him a house like the English had, he would consider giving Smith plenty of food for Jamestown. His additional terms, however, included a gift of English guns. Smith again refused the request. Powhatan seemed to accept Smith's response and gave him baskets of corn to take back to the citizens of Jamestown. By the time the English barges had been loaded, night had fallen and the tide made it impossible to sail. Smith and his party settled in for the night in Powhatan's village.

While the Jamestown party was waiting for dinner to be brought to them, they received a surprise visit from Pocahontas. She told her friend John Smith to be on guard. A plan was afoot for the men bringing their dinner to kill the colonists in order to steal their weapons. Pocahontas took a big risk that night, going against her father to secretly warn the English about the possible attack. Smith thanked her and offered her small gifts, which she would not take for fear that the presents would tip her father off as to what she had done. As suddenly as she had appeared, she was gone.

When the would-be attackers showed up with dinner, Smith and his party were on high alert. They gave the men no chance to follow through on their plan. After a long, uneasy night's sleep, the Jamestown party sailed away from the village the next morning, safe because of Pocahontas's warning.

CHAPTER TWO

CAPTURE AND CONVERSION

The evening in the Powhatan village, when she had warned the Jamestown trading party that they were about to be attacked, was the last time Pocahontas was to have contact with Smith for quite a while. It would also mark a break from her visits to the colony. An accident caused him to return to England late in 1609. But the colonists told Pocahontas that Smith had died. Consequently, she did not return to the colony for the next four years.

Powhatan huts, part of a larger re-creation at Virginia's Jamestown Settlement site. Similar huts may have been common in Pocahontas's village.

After Smith's return to England, relations between the colonists and the Native Americans deteriorated. Powhatan began a campaign to starve the English out of Virginia. The tribes under his rule stopped bartering for food and carried out attacks on English parties that came in search of trade. Hunting became highly dangerous, as the Indians killed Englishmen they found outside the fort. Long reliant on the Indians, the colony found itself with far too little food for the winter. That period has been commonly known as the Starving Time.

In a message to Chief Powhatan the following May, the new governor of Jamestown, Thomas West, demanded that the chief return some stolen English tools and weapons and also turn over the perpetrator of the recent murder of an Englishman. Powhatan replied with "proud and disdainful answers" (as one colonist put it), telling West to either keep the colonists within the Jamestown peninsula or leave the country. The exchange brought about a state of war between the Indians and the English that lasted several years.

AN UNWILLING BARGAINING CHIP

While she was still in her early teens, Pocahontas caught the attention of Captain Samuel Argall. Employed by the Virginia Company, Argall originally was commissioned in 1609 to discover a shorter route to Virginia and to fish for sturgeon. In 1610 he was named admiral of Virginia. In his travels he had become acquainted with Japazeus, a member of the Patawomeck tribe. The Patawomeck were located along the Potomac River, beyond Chief Powhatan's empire. In March 1613, while trading for corn along the river, Argall learned that Pocahontas was staying with Japazeus. He quickly hatched a plan to kidnap the Powhatan princess and

Pocahontas, by Robert Matthew Sully. Few images of Pocahontas were made in her lifetime, so later artists, such as Sully, had to use their imaginations when painting her.

use her as a bargaining chip against her father. His goal was to win back colonists that had been captured by the Indians, as well as several weapons that had been taken during attacks in and around Jamestown. Furthermore, he hoped that he could get a large stockpile of corn, to replenish the colony's pitiful supply of food.

Argall convinced Japazeus and his wife to lure Pocahontas onto his ship. According to historian David Price, their plan was for the husband and wife to walk with the Powhatan princess past Argall's ship, which was anchored off the shore of the Potomac River. Japazeus's wife would fake a desire to go on board, claiming she was curious. Knowing of Pocahontas's fondness for the English and her own

THE VIRGINIA COMPANY

The full name of the Virginia Company was the Virginia Company of London. It was a commercial trading company, chartered by King James I of England in April 1606. Its shareholders were Londoners, and it was distinguished from the Plymouth Company, which was chartered at the same time and composed largely of men from Plymouth, in southwestern England. The Virginia Company had been set up for the purpose of colonizing the eastern coast of North America. Not only that, but stockholders hoped to convert the natives of the Americas to Christianity as they opened new areas for trade. With regard to gaining land, the English were competing with the Spanish, who already had colonized what is now Florida.

curiosity, they were convinced she would go with them aboard the ship.

Their trick worked. Argall showed his visitors around the ship and even gave them supper. Afterward, however, when it came time for the natives to go back to shore, the captain refused to let Pocahontas leave. He called her his "honored guest," but Pocahontas knew those were just words. She was Argall's prisoner.

The captain sent a messenger to Chief Powhatan with his demands. Although Powhatan met one of Argall's conditions by releasing seven English prisoners, he did not

A scene showing Pocahontas as a captive. This painting probably shows her arrival at Henricus, weeks after she had been held on Captain Samuel Argall's ship.

The Baptism of Pocahontas, by John Chapman, illustrates Pocahontas's conversion to Christianity. The English hoped to convert all the natives who lived in the New World.

return the weapons and tools that Argall claimed had been stolen from the colonists. Negotiations broke down after that when Powhatan refused to bargain further.

RELIGIOUS CONVERSION AND MARRIAGE

Once negotiations had come to a standstill, Pocahontas was taken to an English outpost called Henricus, near present-day Richmond, Virginia. There she was treated with courtesy during her captivity. In keeping with the English desire to Christianize the Native Americans, Pocahontas was soon given a religious education, in addition to lessons on English dress and customs. Pocahontas eventually adopted the ways of her captors, though she may have had

An artist's interpretation of Pocahontas's wedding to John Rolfe. Settlers and Indians are shown in attendance, indicating that the union had the blessing of English and Native American leaders alike.

little choice in the matter. Before too long she had become a convert to Christianity. When she was baptized, she took the English name Rebecca.

Religion was not the only thing Pocahontas found while living among the English in Henricus. There she met John Rolfe, a young widower noted as the first colonist to grow tobacco as a crop. In 1614 he requested permission to marry Pocahontas. Governor Thomas Dale readily agreed. Powhatan also was pleased by the proposal and sent an envoy to the wedding. The couple was married on April 5, 1614, in the Anglican church at Jamestown. As the colony's leaders had hoped, following the marriage, peace prevailed between the English and the Indians as long as Powhatan lived.

In 1615, Rebecca and John Rolfe's only child, Thomas, was born. The next year the family, with several Indian attendants, sailed to England for a visit.

CHAPTER THREE

LIFE IN ENGLAND

In the spring of 1616, Pocahontas, her husband, their one-year-old son, Thomas, and a group of Native American men and women sailed with Governor Dale to England. Some sources have reported that among those in the traveling party was another of Powhatan's daughters, Matachanna. Pocahontas's sister supposedly was along as Thomas's nanny. Matachanna's husband, Tomocomo, went as well, with orders to report back to Powhatan all he had seen and heard in England. Coincidentally, they set sail on *The Treasurer*—the vessel on which Pocahontas had been held captive three years before. Her captor, Samuel Argall, was the ship's captain.

It was the British who proposed the trip in the first place. The Virginia Company apparently saw the visit as a way to publicize the colony and to win support from King James I and investors. It also didn't hurt that Pocahontas was a living, breathing success story for English efforts to Christianize the natives of America.

J. W. Glass's imagining of Pocahontas and her husband, John Rolfe. After their son, Thomas, was born, the family traveled to England.

DRESSED TO THRILL

While living among the English, Pocahontas is said to have dressed as they did. Notice how this painting also makes her facial features look like those of an English lady.

Wherever she went, Pocahontas dressed and acted as if she was English nobility, not Indian royalty. (Like the bulk of the trip, her wardrobe was financed by the Virginia Company.) The same could not always be said of the other Native Americans in her traveling party. The others wore clothes closer to what they would wear at home in the Americas. They applied colorful paint to their exposed skin and stuck feathers in their hair. Pocahontas's brother-in-law outdid them all. Reportedly, his face was painted as well as his arms, and his long, dark hair was pulled back in a ponytail. Witnesses later claimed, with equal measures of awe and shock, that he wore the skins and body parts of animals as accessories.

TALK OF THE TOWN

According to several accounts, the English were delighted with Pocahontas. She was the guest of honor at several parties and grand events, including plays and balls. The bishop of London received, or welcomed, her with all the proper ceremony and great respect due a princess—even one who used to be a "savage."

Pocahontas was believed to have been entertained at royal festivities as well. Reliable accounts mention that she was introduced to the king when she attended what would nowadays be considered a piece of participatory

Although Pocahontas is shown above being presented at the court of King James, after whom Jamestown had been named, some historians do not believe she was ever received at court.

theater called a Twelfth Night masque. The show, staged in observance of the twelve days of Christmas, was written by celebrated English playwright Ben Jonson. There also was a popular story that King James and Queen Anne received her and members of her party at the palace. There are people who doubt this occurred, given the source.

The origin of the story about privately meeting the royals rests squarely with an old friend, Captain John Smith. When he discovered that Pocahontas would be traveling to England, Smith supposedly took it upon himself to write a letter to the queen. The content of the letter was about how Pocahontas had saved his life—twice—and what a good friend she had been to the queen's subjects living in Jamestown. He finished by respectfully requesting that her majesty herself make sure that this loyal friend of the crown be treated like the royalty she was. Queen Anne may or may not have had a hand in making sure Pocahontas was treated well. But historians are pretty sure the Indian princess never received an audience with England's royals, despite Smith's story that said otherwise.

SAVIOR AND SAVED MEET AGAIN

Smith found that he could not pass up the opportunity to visit with Pocahontas while she was in England. Shortly before she was set to return to Virginia, he went to call upon her where she was staying outside of London. The meeting did not begin well. Smith later recalled that Pocahontas had greeted him rather coolly, then, without saying another word, turned her face from him as if she was annoyed or upset. She might have been angry that it took Smith so long to come see her. Perhaps she was overwhelmed at seeing her former friend alive after she had thought him dead for so long. (She hadn't learned that the captain was still among the living until a few weeks before their meeting.)

Whatever the reason, she appeared distraught. Smith and her husband chose to leave her alone for a while, to see if her mood would change. Eventually Pocahontas allowed the visit to continue, but neither she nor Smith

A postcard featuring John Smith and Pocahontas. Smith is shown wearing what he might have worn in Jamestown, while Pocahontas is dressed as she would have been in England.

A monument to Pocahontas in Gravesend, England, where she died while attempting to return to Virginia. Historians now estimate that she was not much older than twenty-one when she died.

seemed to get back the feeling of kinship they shared when the princess was a child. Still, seeing her again seems to have had a positive effect on him. It was during her stay in London that Smith revised the book on his Virginia experiences to include the story of the first time Pocahontas had rescued him.

ILLNESS AND DEATH

In 1617 the Rolfes prepared to return to Virginia. While preparing to return to America, Pocahontas fell ill, probably with lung disease but perhaps with smallpox. Her illness took a turn for the worse and interrupted her return voyage before her ship left the River Thames. She died in the town of Gravesend at about age twenty-one and was buried there on March 21, 1617. Afterward her husband immediately returned to Virginia; her son remained in England until 1635, when he went to Virginia and became a successful tobacco planter.

CHAPTER FOUR

LASTING INFLUENCE

Those people who make their mark on history are subject to becoming part of a legend. Resembling folktales in content, legends may include supernatural beings, elements of mythology, or explanations of natural phenomena. They differ from folktales, however, in that they are popularly regarded as historical, even though they are not entirely verifiable. In other words, legends often start out as stories about a real-life person or event. But as time goes by, and the story gets retold many times, the facts may be added to or changed, to make the story more dramatic and larger than life.

The Jamestown Colony has, in many ways, become shrouded in legend. The founding of the Jamestown Colony and early years have been the subject of numerous novels, dramas, and motion pictures—many of them highly fanciful. Pocahontas, especially, has fallen victim to this type of re-creation and reimagining. Then there is the matter of John Smith's mythic description of his rescue by Pocahontas, which has been accepted by some as history, although no one knows for sure whether or not it is true.

Because she was a princess, Pocahontas may have worn elaborate buckskin and feathers when she got older. But such things were not necessarily worn by Native Americans, especially children.

It can be hard to figure out what is fact and what is fact-plus-fiction in stories about Pocahontas. We only have the words of a handful of others—through colonists' letters and diaries, and the accounts of John Smith—to paint a picture of who she was. But reviewing these stories can reveal a glimpse of the true Pocahontas, and help us determine her influence on history and the legacy she has left.

IMAGES OF POCAHONTAS

The way Pocahontas is portrayed often changes to suit whoever is telling her story. This is understandable, because it is easy for artists and writers to interject a little bit of themselves or their vision of the world into everything they create. Also, when little is known about a particular part of Pocahontas's life, people are sometimes left to fill in the gaps with reasonable assumptions or known facts about others like her.

For instance, consider her physical appearance and the way in which she dressed. In American literature and art, Pocahontas most often is seen as a stereotypical "Indian princess." She is shown wearing a modest buckskin dress, with a feather or two stuck in her flowing black hair. The truth, which can be gathered from colonial writings, is that at the time she was visiting Jamestown as a child, Pocahontas typically was almost completely naked. Powhatan children did not wear much clothing until they reached a certain age.

There is only one known image of Pocahontas that was created while she was alive. The engraving, completed by

Simon van de Passe in 1616, shows her dressed in European clothing, including a bulky jacket with a large lace collar. A single feather sticks out from the band of her hat, and some of her black hair is visible. Despite the way she is dressed, she still has facial features that indicate she is Native American.

Simon van de Passe's engraving of Pocahontas is the only known likeness that the Native American princess posed for and that was completed in her lifetime.

In the journey from de Passe's engraving to how she appears in a painting by John Gadsby Chapman (*The Baptism of Pocahontas*, 1836), Pocahontas's features and skin tone became dramatically different. In later works, she more closely resembles European and European-American concepts of human beauty, with whiter skin and lighter-colored hair.

FAMED IN SONG AND STORY

Pocahontas has even found her way into popular music. In 1958, singer Peggy Lee had a hit with a song titled "Fever." The lyrics included these lines:

> Cap'n Smith and Pocahontas
> Had a very mad affair
> When her daddy tried to kill him
> She said, "Daddy, oh don't you dare!"

Decades later, Canadian singer-songwriter Neil Young sang about Pocahontas on his album *Rust Never Sleeps* (1979). The lyrics cast her as an object of romantic desire living in an unspoiled America.

Finally, in 1995, moviegoers across America came out of theaters singing "Colors of the Wind," which was featured in the animated film *Pocahontas.* The song was also a Top 40 radio hit, sung by Vanessa Williams.

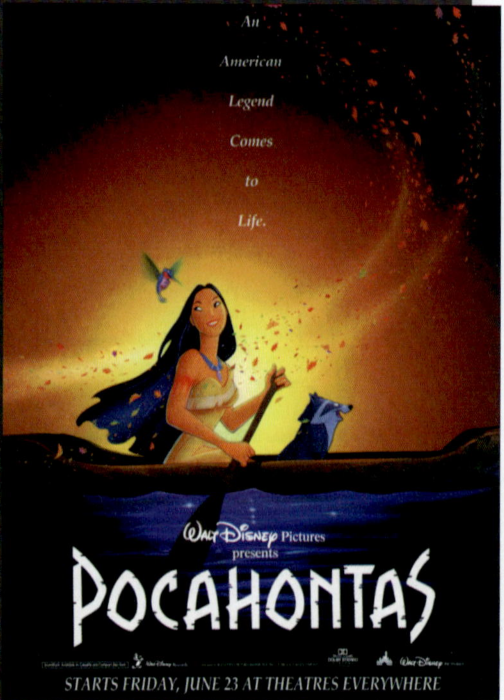

Pocahontas received "the Disney treatment" when Disney made an animated musical of her life–complete with animal friends and a romance with John Smith.

INTERRACIAL MARRIAGE

Throughout history, Pocahontas's story has often been refashioned to serve the purposes of those interpreting it. Beginning in the early nineteenth century, for instance, much emphasis was placed on Pocahontas's interracial marriage with John Rolfe. According to cultural historians, several pre-Civil War abolitionists claimed Pocahontas as a symbol of the possibility of racial harmony. Southerners of that time, however, often glossed over the issue of "racial mixing" in order to hold the Rolfes up as original members of the Southern aristocracy—after all, Pocahontas was both a native Virginian and a princess. This fit their vision of Americans springing from noble, privileged roots rather than from impoverished Pilgrims, which was the slant they felt Northerners generally favored.

Many people like to trace their ancestry in an attempt to see if they are related to somebody famous. Early in the 1900s, many influential Virginians claimed to have found some connection to Pocahontas. They traced their roots back to Thomas Rolfe, who had returned to the area after his mother's death and later started a family. While this connection helped secure the social status of some prominent whites in Virginia society, there was a problem. In 1924, Virginia had passed a "racial purity" law aimed at forbidding interracial marriage, so as to not have people with "mixed blood." So how could whites be against mixed-race children while proudly proclaiming to be related to a person of color?

Virginia decided to enact what became known as the Pocahontas Exception. This law stated that people who

Jamestown map, created from John Smith's stories, featuring Powhatan (*left*) and an Indian warrior (*right*). Noticeably absent is Pocahontas, who has figured prominently in various other accounts of the settlement.

were only one-sixteenth Native American were still considered legally white. A connection to Pocahontas could then be made using that blood percentage or less, and those claiming to be related to her would be exempt from restrictions placed on full-blooded Native Americans, people of color, or those with higher percentages of mixed blood. Certain prominent families could boast of a link to Pocahontas without having to suffer any negative consequences.

PROFOUND EFFECT OF A PRINCESS

With Pocahontas's death in 1617, relations between the Jamestown colonists and the Native Americans started a downward slide, and they eventually broke down completely a few years after her father died in 1618. While sad, these events only serve to prove that the life of the Powhatan princess had a profound effect on the survival of the colony. Likewise, her marriage to Rolfe and trip to England helped keep interest in Jamestown, and English colonization of the New World in general, alive and well. In ways big and small, Pocahontas truly was a woman who changed history.

GLOSSARY

bartering The act of exchanging one commodity (saleable item) for another.

charter A grant or guarantee of rights, franchises, or privileges from the sovereign power of a state or country.

colony A body of people living in a new territory but retaining ties with the parent state.

confederacy A league or compact for mutual support or common action.

convert To change from one belief, view, or party to another; or a person who has been converted.

diplomacy Skill in handling affairs or conducting negotiations without arousing hostility.

distraught The state of being upset or suffering extreme mental conflict or pain.

envoy A person delegated to represent one government in its dealings with another.

famine A condition wherein there is no food for people to eat.

founding Taking the first steps to build something.

impoverished Poor.

interject To throw in between or among other things.

intimidation Using fear to make someone do something.

peninsula A portion of land nearly surrounded by water and connected with a larger body by a narrow strip of land.

phenomena Observable facts or events.

replenish To fill or build up again.

resumption The act of resuming, or picking something up again.

sturgeon A type of bony freshwater fish found primarily in northern climates.

subsequent Following in time, order, or place; coming after.

suppressed Being put down by authority or force.

FOR FURTHER READING

Doherty, Brian. *The Story of Pocahontas*. New York, NY: Dover Publications, 2012.

Fay, Gail. *Pocahontas*. Chicago, IL: Heinemann, 2014.

Jenner, Caryn. *The Story of Pocahontas*. London, UK: DK Children, 2012.

Lusted, Marcia Amidon. *The Jamestown Colony Disaster: A Cause-and-Effect Investigation*. Minneapolis, MN: Lerner Publications, 2016.

Mattern, Joanne. *Pocahontas*. New York, NY: Scholastic, 2015.

Rajczak, Kristen. *The Life of Pocahontas*. New York, NY: PowerKids Press, 2016.

Sewall, Marcia. *James Towne: Struggle for Survival*. New York, NY: Atheneum Books, 2014.

Wight Edmunds, Pocahontas. *The Pocahontas-John Smith Story*. New York, NY: Firework Press, 2015.

WEBSITES

Because of the changing nature of internet links, Rosen Publishing has developed an online list of websites related to the subject of this book. This site is updated regularly. Please use this link to access this list:

http://www.rosenlinks.com/WWCH/pocahontas

INDEX